AMERICA'S

CW01507630

Drummond G Marvin

AMERICA'S 51st STATE

Drummond G Marvin

America's 51st State

by

Drummond G Marvin

(Not an Historian)

(To be taken with a pinch of salt)

(The author 'to be taken' etc. …not the book!)

(Buy it, please!)

AMERICA'S 51st STATE

Copyright © 2019 Drummond G Marvin

ISBN: 9781688699205

ALL RIGHTS RESERVED

OBLIGATORY INTRODUCTION

On 21st July 1933 the author was born, in Scotland.

At only six months old he was taken to England, by his parents (obviously, he couldn't go by himself.)

He has lived and worked in that country taking his English Father's Nationality and cheering on that country's rugby team - even watching cricket!

During his retirement he and his wife emigrated to Spain and the sun.

For the want of something better to do, he took to writing letters to the Editors of the Local and National papers; about any subject that took his fancy. One or two were published.

From the following correspondence you will see that England and Wales conjoined to become the 51st State of America.

The author's first letter of many was addressed to 'The Editor of the Costa Blanca News' and was ignored. Somewhat astonished at this rejection, it was then submitted to the editor of the 'Oldie' magazine.

He sent another and another but had to get in touch by the old fashioned telephone method, to alert the Editor's Office of what they were missing.

I used the phrase 'old fashioned' because at the time of writing communications have advanced beyond our wildest dreams. This is to be expected, because we are in the latter half of the 21st century; the date being April 2064.

The letters that follow lead to a conclusion which a few won't be satisfied with, but many may very well be.

Where necessary editor's notes will explain them but, all in all, the story should unfold in the reading.

CONTENTS

AMERICA'S 51st STATE

AMERICA'S 51st STATE
1 April 2064
Unpublished letter to the Editor
Costa Blanca News

Dear Sir,

I would like to take this opportunity to wish all my fellow ex-pat American citizens, living in Spain, a very happy Easter. As you know we have almost reached a milestone: to-day being 1st April 2064, we are exactly 22 days away from a very important celebration.

May I remind you of some of the momentous achievements and decisions made during these past sixty-four years? The 21st century began with Great Britain, conjoined with Europe, steadily seeing its influence draining away. In 2016 a referendum resulted in a motion to break-away from the Union and three and a half years later, on 19th March 2020 negotiations were incomplete and we hadn't left; still with the same old markets.

It is important to mention at this time, an incident that occurred which advanced the world's culture beyond our wildest imagination. More will be made of this later but suffice to say, it all began when Hillary Clinton, the Democratic Candidate for the US Presidency, had her e-mail and other online correspondence hacked by Russia. In retaliation the out-going incumbent, Barack Obama, swamped the airwaves with cybernetics. This 'cyber' activity was returned by Russia and finally China joined in. The result of all these lines of communication, bumping into each other, led to a major scientific discovery; which I will speak about later, as promised.

On a personal note, the writers' club I belong to in Murcia was founded in 2008 and styled 'Wordplay'. In 2016 the name was changed to 'Writers' Ink' and that was intended to be our final identification. However in 2020 and thanks to a legacy, kindly left to us by our founder Michael Barton, we became incorporated and now have to call ourselves 'Writers Ink Inc'. (We may have to have a rethink.)

Anyway I digress. In 2017 Donald Trump took office and served his first term surprisingly well. He became almost every tyrant's friend and Great Britain provided a safe haven for his meetings with world leaders; a half-way house if you like. He and Putin were never off his golf courses in Scotland.

The general rule was that each country or group of countries, holding the Presidency for a 4 year term, must have a population in excess of 8. 5 million. Their 'SOD' (Seat(s) of Deliberations) could be shared. (e.g. Austria (pop: 8,238,610) - I year at The Rathaus of Vienna; Liechtenstein (pop: 37,461) – 1 year in the Prince's Castle, Vaduz: The Holy See (pop: 800) – I year in the Vatican and Sark (pop: more sheep than people) – 1 year at the Seigneur's bungalow, 13 Guernsey View. There was no problem at the first three venues but it was a bit of a crush at 13 Guernsey Avenue for the 4 Presidents and their 200 strong travelling circuses.

One major edict was passed, when this group were in collective office. All petrol driven vehicles were to be scrapped within ten years from date of enactment. (This meant all vehicles in the world were to be re-cycled by 2032.) For those interested in the reasons behind legislation then they should be told this had nothing to do with supporting a 'Clean Air' bill. It was as a result of a social interlude, held in the Prince's armoury in his castle at Vaduz, when the Seigneur of Sark happened to express a nostalgic preference for the good-old days. He mentioned no petrol driven vehicles were allowed on the roads of Sark; a couple of electric golf buggies sufficed. The air was pure. It was this that impressed the Crown Prince and the Pope. (But they hadn't spent their year at 13, Guernsey View yet!)

Again I have run out of time. In my next letter I will let you know the consequences of this waste disposal programme. Hopefully we will be a step nearer the reason for my writing these letters.

Drummond Gordon Marvin.

Letter No. 2 - 2 April 2064

Dear Sir,

Apropos my letter dated 1st April, 2064 and, as promised therein, I would like to reveal the exciting new scientific discovery I mentioned to all your readers. Please forgive me if my explanation leaves you a little confused as I too find it hard to understand. The only scientific teaching I received was when I was hit over the head with Steven Hawkin's book, 'A Life in Science': second edition.

Before revealing this closely guarded innovation certain checks and balances have to be undergone to ensure its veracity. I can tell you, however, what it is not. It isn't the recent discovery The Elixir of Life. Old age pensions commence now at 140 years of age. The Chelsea Old Age Pensioners are now referred to as 'The Very Old Age Pensioners.'

For those who didn't read my first letter, mention was made of the cybernetic traffic criss-crossing the Atlantic Ocean betwixt and between the United States of America and Russia. Saturation point resulted in these radio waves crashing into each other and returning from whence they had come. The Americans resented receiving communications telling them, "Y'all get stuffed now. Have a nice day." Even though they thought it vaguely familiar they secretly admired the phraseology. It later dawned upon them that they'd been receiving their own messages back!

Hardly anything remained a secret for long, except for 'Who was the antagonist in the Mousetrap?' Will it ever close?

These cybernetics took a few years to run their course – however 'every cloud etc. …' and not long after this time (2017 – 2021) Austria, Liechtenstein (twinned with the Isle of Sark) and the Holy See, collectively took over the Presidency of '**TWERPS**' - (**T**he **W**orld **E**xecutives' **R**otatory **P**arliamentary **S**eat). Every four years a different country or countries would take-over and could legislate 'willy nilly' without fear or favour. (n.b.This organisation was originally known as 'The World's Administrative Temporary Seat'.)

Towards the end of 2024 – Trump's supposedly final four year stint - Congress voted a change to the Constitution to allow him a further term of office; he had become so popular. During this 3rd term (2025 – 2028) the term 'Brexit' was rapidly reverting to 'Brentry'. So, England and Wales conjoined to become the 51st State of the United States of America. His Majesty, the very elderly, King George VII, (LATTERLY Prince Charles, The Prince of Wales), became The Governor of this new founded State. There were three Senators appointed to represent England (North, Central and South), and two for Wales (North and South). The Senator for England Central being 'oldie' Nigel Farrage.

With the exception of Barron, who was more interested in running a plastic conglomerate, the American Presidency soon became the fiefdom of the family Trump. In 2029 Ivanka, aged 47, took over from her father to be followed in 2041 by Tiffany until 2048 (Only did two terms) and then Eric, aged 64, and finally in 2062 we are back with Donald Trump, 84, but this time it is 'the junior'.

Next time I will tell you about the wonderful advances to science Cyber activity has produced. Until then have a nice day, as we now say!

Drummond G Marvin
Murcia, Spain
(Full name and address supplied)

(Ed. Note. I know Farrage is normally spelled with one 'R', but doing it this way in the text - he can't sue!)
D.G.M

Letter No. 3 - 3rd April 2064

Dear Sir,

Apropos my previous two letters – and I promise never to use that 'apropos' word again - dated 1st & 2nd April 2064. As mentioned therein, I would like to reveal the exciting new 'scientific discovery', spoken of, to all your readers; providing they're all sitting comfortably?
I would like to… but at this moment in time it would be foolish of me to reveal it. Much better to show the various steps leading up to this 'Scientific Celebratory American Miracle'. It's almost too good to be true. Various factors played a part in its development; these 'stepping-stones', leading to its end result, should be identified - for greater clarification.

In 2020 before leaving their '**TWERP**' (see letter No: 2), at the Vatican, an edict was passed for the 'Scrapping of all Petrol Driven Vehicles' (in the World) This was a year earlier than anticipated so, bearing in mind the time stipulation imposed, all vehicles (including the Pope's mobile) would have to be converted to either electricity or solar power by 2030. It took a lot longer because it had its problems
.

As far as the oil is concerned we're not talking about millions of tonnes, or even trillions but perhaps millions of trillions. Where were we going to store it all, prior to destruction? How were we going to get rid of it? Bury it, burn it, lose it? Finally some Nobel Prize winner (in literature) suggested evaporation! That became the buzz word! After our initial euphoria the question 'where' raised its ugly head. If all the refineries in the entire world had to be emptied, it would require a country the size of Brasil to accommodate it all. Well, in the end, we settled on its rain forest part, to take in the condemned fuel in stages. Still the Brasilians were none too happy.

Mobilisation of forces was called for. So the appointed leaders of the **N.H.I.T.S.** and **S.H.I.T.S.** (**N**orthern & **S**outhern **H**emisphere's **I**mpugnable **T**reaty **S**tructure) drew up plans for the evacuation and repatriation of all Brasilians not actively engaged in the rain forest.
Ed note: The N. Hemisphere had more members.

Why Brasil you may ask. North Korea had been suggested as well as Scotland but there are no mangrove swamps in either of those two locations. It would seem from past experience that a 1,000 tonnes per year of crude oil discharged to a low-energy mangrove swamp will have a much different impact than the same 1,000 tonnes per year released into the deep waters of the Korea Bay or the North Sea.

In my next letter I will explain how we accomplished these tasks; satisfactorily I might add.

Drummond G Marvin

Letter No. 4 - 4 April 2050

Dear Sir,

Continuing the story so far, but before revealing this exciting new discovery and putting it to the test, let me bring a conclusion to the disposal of the oil and petrol saga mentioned earlier (see 3rd Letter).

The choice of Brasil had its problems. There were mango swamps but not to the required acreage; the rain forest had to go. In itself this was to our advantage, as the wood so obtained offset the lack of alternative fuel sources.

Once levelled the dumping began. Special solar powered container vehicles were used to collect the condemned fuel from the World's giant tankers; some was dropped from the new 'TBizer' aircraft. (Turbine driven.)

The Brasilian rain forest workers showed remarkable tolerance throughout. Rioting had been anticipated but instead a 'slap happy' attitude was displayed. Of course sniffing gasoline is an easy way for people to temporarily escape their problems; it can also help relieve boredom.

We, at **TWERPS**, could have done with a sniff or two but the different toxins involved could have a devastating effect on the body long-term.

Evaporation became our main concern. As everyone knows (Certainly Merv F Fingas does) evaporation of a liquid can be considered as the movement of molecules from the surface into the vapour phase above it. The air boundary layer is immediately above the evaporation surface. Under conditions where the air boundary layer doesn't move (no wind) or has low turbulence, the air immediately above the water quickly becomes saturated and evaporation slows.
This problem was solved by sectioning this Amazon dumping area off into 1,000 x 1,000 square mile units, each surrounded by wind machines serviced by wind turbines. These had been manufactured using all the metal from the crushed vehicles, redundant oil derricks, pumps etc. It took about five years for this method to take effect BUT where had the toxin vapours gone to?

Rainfall provided the clue, as it had a slightly oily consistency. The 'Mediterranean Look' was common, even among Ethiopians! However there were dangers especially to our monthly space shuttle trips to Mars. Space craft were all designated 'non-smoking 'craft. I hate to think what would have happened if someone lit a match as he was travelling through the

Tropopause; with the window open? Planet Earth would adopt a burning halo. Uranus and all our settlers would be toast.

(Editor's Note: Venus is closer to earth but doesn't sound as painful!).

I will have to stop now as I'm becoming a little breathless. This is no doubt due to the demise of the Amazon's rain forest (The Lungs of the Planet) as it can no longer recycle carbon monoxide into oxygen. It had produced 20% of the World's oxygen.
Perhaps that was a 'mistaka' we should not 'hava' made.

In my next letter I will - at last - reveal the new scientific advances made in this half century; and the reason for this preamble.

Drummond G Marvin

Letter No. 5 - 5th April 2064

Dear Sir,

Only 18 days to go before the celebrations begin. Yes, it's a very famous person and the anniversary is important; but who is it and what is the anniversary? 10, 50,100 years or more…? All will be revealed, shortly, should the clues to be given fail to register.

Looking back through the century so far, quite a lot has been accomplished and, for the benefit of those who missed any of my previous letters, a quick re-cap would be in order.

The new century commenced with Great Britain (including Northern Ireland) firmly ensconced as a fully-fledged member of the European Union.

In 2016, and for reasons too numerous to itemise, the Prime Minister of the day held a referendum which resulted in a vote to break-away from Europe. As a result of this vote the Prime Minister was replaced by another from his party. It was agreed that a cessation from Europe, without resumption, would occur by March 2019.

For most of 2016/17 the good people of America were deciding between candidates for their Presidency. It became a 'two horse' race between Hillary Clinton of the Democratic Party and Donald Trump for the Republicans. It would appear that attempts to influence the election in favour of Trump were made by Russia hacking the email accounts of Hillary Clinton and others.

To combat this, CIA and FBI reciprocated in like manner and soon the cybernetics became uncontrollable.

On 20th January 2017 Trump was inaugurated as the 45th President of the United States of America.

On 19th March, 2019 Great Britain should have become independent from Europe but the politicians couldn't reach a consensus. We were still beholden to the Court of European Justice et al.

Trump's tenure was extended until 2028 and during this time (2027) England and Wales became America's 51st State. England returned Nigel Farrage as one of its three Senators. Scotland and Northern Ireland applied to remain in the European Union.

Wiki Leaks exposed the killer in the Mousetrap and they were hacked and bugged out of business – a leak too far!

During Trump's first term he and Putin of Russia met frequently in Reykjavik, Iceland to discuss the World's problems.

Nigel Farrage was present as he had shown Putin a good time, whilst he was visiting Great Britain. He hadn't much to offer concerning the world's problems but mentioned that in England the Civil Service were working to rule until they received wages comparable to those of the Southern Rail employees.

As a result of these meetings **TWERPS** (**T**he **W**orld **E**xecutive's **R**otating **P**arliamentary **S**eat(s)) was founded. Country (...ies) with populations of or in excess of 8.5 million would govern by rotation for a period of 4 years. They would pass laws to be obeyed instantly.

About 2021 Austria, Liechtenstein, the Holy See (Vatican) and The Isle of Sark conjoined in this World Government. They passed the law abolishing the use of petrol and oil. All petrol driven vehicles and machinery had to be scrapped and the fuel destroyed. The problems this caused would take too long to itemise but it would be remiss of me to ignore them completely.

The Rain Forest in Brasil was chosen as the dumping ground and all the trees and vegetation cut from their roots.

The giant Kapok Tree, with its 10 ft. diameter trunk, had to go. It was still used though, while stocks lasted in its dead form, for the three 'Cs' – Carvings, Coffins and Canoes. BUT timber as an alternative fuel source produced innumerable problems as I will explain in my next letter.

Drummond G Marvin

Letter No. 6 - 6th April, 2064

Dear Sir,

Timber was running out fast. Trees were becoming more and more expensive and within ten years 'wood' replaced the 'gold standard'. It became the 'Timber Standard' and topped $2,000 an ounce; depending on the type of wood, of course. For example: the Pennantia Baylisiana is the only single tree in existence and can be found on one of the three Kings Islands, off the coast of New Zealand; Attenborough's Pitcher Plant, has a few hundred remaining on Mount Victoria, in Palawan, Philippines; and a Suicide Palm, that lives for 50 years in North West Madagascar then dies; when it flowers just once. Its trunk is 18m and height 90m.

The timber prices drop, according to type, quality and availability. The White Oaks and Douglas Firs were more plentiful but even the latter of these was subject to, what was known as, the three 'Fs'. (Firs For Fuel); sometimes referred to as the four 'Fs'!
The rare trees, mentioned above, fashioned the many trophies and awards previously made in gold. The football world cup (Jules Rimet) was first presented in 2022 at Qatar as, unfortunately, the W.C - 'Wood Cup'; the

Cheltenham Timico Gold Cup, in March each year, was also so changed and named; and the Olympic Gold Medals were replaced by wood - the silver also, but of a slightly lower quality. Even dentists were replacing gold implants with 'Pitcher Plant'; unfortunately a sparkling smile became a toothless grin.

A branch of the Pennantia Baylisiana tree was used to produce the Jules Rimet and the Trimico cups. The Suicide Palm was used to replace the Olympic 'golds' and the Coral Tree for the 'silvers'.

Now to remind you of the further advances made long-term. We mentioned the pollution caused by the evaporation of the dumped fuel. It circled the earth and lodged in the Troposphere. Oily rain was the norm. The Mediterranean look prevailed.

Mention was also made of our advanced planet travel. Space craft were being sent monthly to Venus and Mars! Venus was being prepared for long term human habitation but Mars was being adopted as a penal type colony where all the bad people were to be sent – not all Australians, I hasten to add.

I should mention that '**NATO**' had been replaced by '**N. & S.H.I.T.S**.' (**N**orthern and **S**outhern **H**emispheres' **I**mpugnable **T**reaty **S**tructures).

To continue it is now about 2040 and a new industrial revolution has taken place.

Unemployment has reached maximum capacity. Think tanks from both hemispheres came to the conclusion that 'Robots' were the cause. These man made machines had been given too much intelligence. They had started to think for themselves and could take different routes to achieve a result if they had prior knowledge of a faulty path previously tried. They didn't need telling.

This came to the fore when they (robots) formed their own union! They wanted to strike whenever their minders (humans) forgot to butter their machinery. (There was no oil available) They liked Kerry Gold – or should that be renamed now?

Drummond G Marvin

Letter No.7 - 7 April 2064

Dear Sir,

Timothy Noel Thynk, Emeritus Professor of Artificial Intelligence (Scientific) at the University of Silicon Valley; B.Sc. (Hon) Camb; Ph.D(Just!)Yale and 3 x 'As' & 2 x 'Cs' in School Cert (Shoreditch Sec: Mod:), and presently a 'Cryogenicist at the Cryonics Institute USA, had just finished lunch and was listening to an information 'sound bite', emanating from the restaurant's serving robot waiter's wrist watch.
The snatch came from a 'Science Today' programme and it repeated what had been said about robots being too intelligent for their own good. 'They could take different routes to achieve a result if they had prior knowledge of a faulty path previously tried. They didn't need telling.'

This got Thynk thinking. Now his own television set could do something similar. But back in the twenties, although you could still use 'catch-up' TV to see programmes lost, if you experienced 'scrambling', 'catch-up' would still repeat this interruption.
Not so now. The programme would be shown in its entirety without the scrambling.

TNT (as Thynk was known to his students, for frequently going off at tangents) progressed with this line of thought and extended it into the field of Cryogenics. Could a human body and mind be brought back to life or even the scrambled form of state they had experienced when alive?

Thynk was well versed in Cryotherapy, which is the use of hyper-cool temperatures to accelerate healing in soft tissue, joints and to increase metabolism. Metals etc, like brakes and rotors, could have their life expectancy lengthened if placed in chambers at 300 degrees below zero.

However, Cryopreservation had his undivided attention. This was the preservation of humans and animals, in liquid nitrogen and or hydrogen, with the intention of future revival.

This liquid Hydrogen and nitrogen provided the fuel for rockets. (Liquid Oxygen was used mainly as an oxidizer). NASA's space shuttles used oxyogenic (hydrogen/oxygen) propellant as a primary means of getting into orbit.
The Russians called it 'Liquefied Natural Gas'. Anyway I digress.

Professor Thynk's deliberations commenced back in the thirties and his experiments, laboratory tests and grave defilements occurred up until the Eureka moment in 2060 when his goal was achieved.

During this time an entire Mammalian brain had been frozen and recovered. The cryogenically preserved brain belonged to a rabbit and using 'Aldehyde-stabilized Cryopreservation' it had been able to return the brain to near-perfect condition.

To cut a long story short, and without having to reveal confidential industrial secrets, certain equipment was manufactured the like of which had never been seen before.
The whole purpose of the Professor's work was to devise a means of reviving and talking to the dead.

To achieve this result:

(a) The person had to be dead, not previously embalmed and easily located by accurate grid coordinates.

(b) Other requirements involved: a vascular filler phase gun;

(c) a Neutron & Snapse Hypodermic Restorer;

(d) space satellite;

(e) a grave digger!

Cryopreservation wasn't ideal as it led to dehydration and destruction of neural connections.

Whilst the rabbit's brain, mentioned, cannot be revived yet, the research suggests all neural components responsible for forming one's personal identity – including memory and personality, can be preserved.

DO NOT TRY THIS AT HOME.

Drummond G Marvin

Letter No. 8 - 8 April 2064

Dear Sir,

Have you guessed yet? Who's anniversary are we about to celebrate, and why? Well, he was a man of letters, born on 23rd April 1564, St George's Day, almost 500 years ago.
Yes, you'd be right in thinking William Shakespeare. I should say 'almost' because, as you see, we still have 15 days to go before that exact date.

Until we perform the hologram materialisation of the Bard it would be helpful to know what exactly we want from our interview. Can he throw any light on the death of Christopher Marlowe? Did his friend and fellow poet/playwright, fake his own death and write or co-write Shakespeare's work? Did he use Shakespeare's name as a pseudonym? Do any of the other theories ring true? What are the other theories?

Before proceeding, let me assure you that the three dimensional picture (hologram) of the Bard, will not be reproduced in these letters. At the moment we are not sure if our equipment is advanced, to a point where we are able - to put flesh on the bones. We would hate to illustrate our talk with an expressionless but communicative skull.

Another requirement, before any interview takes place, is to gather as much background information as possible. This will mean interviewing other known suspects/witnesses depending on which theory is being pursued. I'm waiting for someone to suggest that Queen Elizabeth knew Marlowe had faked his death and had in fact encouraged him to do so. This would mean her Lord Chamberlain and possibly the whole of her Privy Council were involved as well.

I intend to talk to Sir Francis Walsingham and his cousin (first removed) Sir Thomas Walsingham, who employed Ingram Frizer – Marlowe's alleged killer.
I am unable to talk to Frizer as his exact burial ground is unknown. He lived, though, to a good age, by Elizabethan standards, and in a comfortable fashion. It would seem his benefactor, Sir Thomas and his wife, were beholden to him sufficiently to keep him financially secure until he died, in August 1627.

Once the supporting cast have been interviewed, Queen Elizabeth's examination will precede Shakespeare's. We know where she is (Westminster Abbey - 51.499306°N / 0.127480°W.) Hopefully we will be able to get her and Shakespeare's views concerning these allegations of fakery, plagiarism, parallelism, psychological signatures based on word choices, phraseology etc…

One important consideration is the time available for responses; we haven't got very long. Once the R.M. (responder mechanism) has been transferred the interviewee will only have twenty minutes S.C.M. (satellite converter motion) before we lose all signals. The secret is for the responder to use the 'static' button; one press for 'Yes' and two presses for 'No'. (It will be recorded, in written form, as 'static' or 'static/static').

The facts, as we are presently aware, are as follows: Christopher Marlowe, a playwright of emerging importance, whilst on bail on charges of heresy and atheism, had dinner at the dwelling of one Eleanor Bull, a licensed lodging in Deptford, with three other men. After the mid-day meal these four apparently walked in the gardens but nothing else is known until they returned to the house for supper after some four to six hours. It would seem that after this meal, Marlowe and a man called Ingram Frizer were involved in an argument over the bill, which culminated in Frizer stabbing Marlowe either above or in his right eye and killing him instantly. In front of the coroner's jury, of sixteen men, Frizer claimed self-defence as Marlowe had instigated the attack. He was kept in custody but shortly afterwards, pardoned by Queen Elizabeth.

The inquest had been held in the same house a day after the killing and the coroner officiating was the Queen's own. Dame Eleanor's house being within the verge (12 miles) of the Royal Palace at Nonsuch, where the Queen was in residence at the time, made it his responsibility.

Drummond G Marvin

N.B. Dinner taken at mid-day and supper in the early evening. Daylight hours during dinner and candle light in the evening.

Letter No. 9 - 9 April 2064

Dear Sir,

The facts surrounding Marlowe's death leave room for speculation, to say the least. Was this a regular meeting between friends? What was its purpose? Who arranged it? Why Deptford and why at the dwelling of a person of influence? Were these four men the only guests at dinner/supper? Did Mistress Bull serve the meals or did she have someone to help her? Was Mistress Bull introduced to Marlowe or any of the others? Did she know him? What did the four guests do during the period between dinner and supper? What arrangements had any of them made to return home? How did they get there? Where had they all come from? Was Deptford a central point for all concerned?

Did any of the four men involved, have enough money to pay for both the meals taken by the group? Did they all have the same food? Was there alcohol taken and if so by whom and in what quantity?

What time did it get dark in Deptford? Was Dame Eleanor Bull's dwelling well-lit by candle power, or otherwise, during the hours of darkness? What was the weather like – hot or cold? Where were the nearest theatres or traveller's inns/yards to Eleanor Bull's dwelling? Have there been any reports of a young actor missing for his next day's performance on 31st May that year?

It would seem no servants of the Bull establishment were called to give evidence. Was Dame Bull the only occupant of her premises on that day? All these questions should have been asked at the coroner's court but they weren't. Why not?

Before we go down the road of 'what ifs' it would be of interest to repeat some of the theories surrounding and concerning the death or otherwise of Marlowe. The attached list, headed Marlowe's demise or otherwise (9a), although not exhaustive, gives a fair cross section of the various thoughts on the subject.

Some of the suggestions may seem farfetched but there have been one or two that stretched the imagination so much that they couldn't be included.

For example someone opined that as an amateur magician, Marlowe could have swapped heads with another, in order to protect his identity. Not too much thought had been put in to that idea and it was quickly discarded. It didn't have the legs!

Of all the above questions, that seemingly were not asked at the coroner's court, I think the most interesting was 'what happened between dinner and supper on the day of the incident?'
I will explain my choice for this question later. Suffice to say it would be helpful, at this stage, to set the Elizabethan scene, concerning the ways of life and other considerations.

In his 'Description of England' (1577) William Harrison reported..."We in England devide (sic) our people commonly into four sorts, gentlemen, citizens or burgesses, yeoman, and artificers or labourers." The gentry owned the majority of the land and were by birthright the natural leaders. Their average annual income was £200 - £500. About 70% of the rural population consisted of the vulgar and common sort but their social structure was just as important.

Wealthy people lit their homes with beeswax candles which were expensive; others used candles made from tallow which gave off an unpleasant smell.

The poor made do with rush lights made from rushes dipped in animal fat. As there was no electricity, plays and poetry readings were conducted during daylight hours. However actors were distrusted and regarded as layabouts who did no useful work. From 1572 actors had to hold a licence from a noble. Without such protection actors were liable to arrest for vagrancy.

In the early 16th century actors performed in market squares or inn courtyards but when plays became more popular it became worthwhile to build purpose-built theatres in large towns.

In 1576 James Burbage built his first theatre. Rich people sat on the stage and the poor (groundings) stood in the open air. There were no female actors and boys played women's parts.

Drummond G Marvin

Marlowe's Demise or Otherwise - 9a

1 On 30th May 1593, at Dame Eleanor Bull´s licenced victuallers, Marlowe was killed by Ingram Frizer, over who was to pay the bill

2 Marlowe faked his own death.

3 Marlowe, whilst in exile, using the pseudonym William Shakespeare, and wrote the plays and poems attributable to Shakespeare.

4. Marlowe assisted (in exile) Shakespeare to write his plays and poems.

5 Marlowe attended Dame Eleanor Bull's licenced victuallers for dinner and supper. Between meals his dining companions collected the executed dead body of John Penry, from St Thomas-a-Watering, and substituted it for Marlowe when he escaped.

6 Marlowe escaped and the other three waited for (or went to get) a 'body double' for Marlowe. They killed him by a stab to the head, above the eye, in order to cause the victim's features to become more indistinct because of the blood.

7 It was a government/secret service plot to kill/fake Marlowe's death.

8 Frizer killed Marlowe as he was
compromising, his employer and therefore his own employment, as a result of the Atheism accusations.

9 Marlowe, as a member of the 'School of Night', became aware of Essex's plots against Raleigh. When Skeres was unable to persuade him to keep silent his death was assured.

Letter No. 10 - 10 April 2064

Dear Sir,

When Shakespeare was the topic of conversation, I was able to hold my corner having some knowledge of several of his plays. I knew, for example, that: 'Hamlet' was his longest and as an actor he had taken the part of the 'Ghost' in Act 1 Scene 1. (Or was it Scene 2?); 'Caliban' was the leading role in the 'Tempest' which I had read, as a student, at the Preparatory Academy for the Royal Academy of Dramatic Art, back in the 1950's; then there was that Scottish play by an Elizabethan Playwright with the three witches and their nasty little potions; Henry V and Agincourt and all that; Romeo and Juliet and the balcony scene; Richard III which gave me the hump and the Merchant of Venice – to name but a little of his prodigious output.

Poetry, however, eluded me; I think I had the day off school when that discipline was discussed.
Mention of Shakespeare's sonnets conjured up a vision of a little blue book filled with rhyming poems with a musical twist. When I was eventually introduced to them I could not make head or tail of any. They appeared to rhyme,

when one reached the couplet at the end of each.

There were 154, supposedly in chronological order, all with 14 lines (about 3 with one or two lines missing) and either addressed to: a Young 'Fancy' Man or a 'Dark Lady' and were either autobiographical of Shakespeare or by another poet.

I mention all this because I do not want to give the impression that I am either a scholar or a scholiast. (I hope you don't need a 'scholium' for that?) As for me I wouldn't know the difference between a pentameter and any other gas appliance. Whether you are pro Shakespeare and con Marlowe matters not. What does (matter) though is the true meaning of what is written? We have too many ambiguities methinks.

Back in the 2010s we had The European Convention on Human Rights which was interpreted in so many ways by the courts it was hardly worth the bother of implementing it. The same could almost be said for Shakespeare's sonnets as the Marlovians believe certain of them to be written by Marlowe in an autobiographical vein and argue that if Shakespeare was the author there is nothing in his known history to support what he alludes to in the sonnets.

Another school of thought is that they are both wrong as Shakespeare is merely describing the life and times of his friend and patron the Earl of Southampton.

On down to earth matters a major breakthrough occurred, some ten years ago, which is now having an effect. All plastic bottles and bags that had been the cause of such ecological disasters had been neutralised and found a safe haven. They were all recycled into 'Lego' type, straight and curved slabs and taken to Africa where they were slotted together and laid from North to South as a highway devoid of potholes.

Credit for this inventive infrastructure should go to Donald Trump Senior. In 2028, during his last year in office, he built his Mexican wall by recycling plastic bottles and bags into a liquid form and moulding it into bricks. This idea wasn't developed when it was realised all the Mexicans had to do was melt the construction with flame throwers, car exhausts and the like. Rather than combine plastic with asbestos, Trump plumped for bricks.

Getting back to talking to Shakespeare, if it comes off what will it lead to? Missing persons? Could we find Lord Lucan? I mention this, because, during my 28 year service in the police force, I was one of the four or five officers who held the 'Lucan File'; in other words, during my time at Scotland Yard, I was one of the five who couldn't find him. I had hoped we'd catch him during the year 2034, or thereabouts, when he'd have turned one hundred and the Queen would send him a telegram.

 Finally it would be helpful to mention at least one of the many advances made towards some aspects of life and living. Thanks to the introduction of nuclear diets and the raising of the retirement age to 140 years I am rapidly approaching my 132nd birthday. I should really be lodged in the Old Age Quarter of our city but, for the moment, I prefer to stay at home with my parents.

Drummond G Marvin

Letter No. 11 - 11th April 2064

Dear Sir,

The time for our interview with the 'Bard' is fast approaching. So much has been done already but background interviews are proving harder to obtain. For example, it took twice as long to secure an answer from Queen Elizabeth 1st. She had been buried, on 28th April 1603, in her Grand Father Henry V11's chapel, in Westminster Abbey. Then in 1612 she had been moved, on the instructions of James 1st, to the Lady Chapel itself, where she was finally laid to rest, with her half- sister, Mary 1st, placed on top of her.
(Grid Ref: TQ300795. 51% 29'57.9"N. 0% 7'39.26"W.)

Putting questions to Elizabeth, whilst Mary was within earshot, was bad enough; but her demand to be re-buried on top of Mary prior to answering any questions, was the last straw.
Our raised voices had been sufficient to de-activate the 'Neutron & Snapse Hypodermic Restorer'; (Letter 7) not to mention 'The Verbal to Analog Convertor'.
All in all, I gathered that she (Elizabeth 1st) didn't like her father very much.

Before attempting to deal with the many attempts to question Shakespeare's accomplishments, or take credit for them, I should prepare you (the reader) with as much background information to make your own judgement.

I should remind you however that my credentials for undertaking this task are **'ABYSMAL'**. (**A**ccredited **B**y **Y**esteryear's **S**chool **M**atriculation: **A**verage **L**evel.)

Ed. Note. 5 Credits and three passes.

The information I have obtained has been from both 'pro' and 'con' Shakespeare followers/detractors, of Academic or Scholarly backgrounds. When views are expressed by holders of inferior quality, then they will be pre-faced with the mnemonic **ABYSMAL**.

The information that follows is contained in two documents headed (1) 'Shake-speare's Sonnets' and (2) a 'Time Line 1542 – 1616'. You will see the title of the first document is hyphenated to satisfy those who believe some of the contents to be the work of others.

Ed. Note. Abysmal thinking re Shake-speare.

All this information will be transferred onto a micro-dot and fired and absorbed into Will Shakespeare's skull. When we later ask him questions such as:- 'In 1593 the poem Venus and Adonis was published under your name. Was this Christopher Marlowe's work?' or 'Are the Sonnets printed in chronological order?'

 By all means read and digest No. 1 – 'Document on the Sonnets' but as far as No. 2 – 'The Time Line' is concerned use it for reference purposes only, as it is intended to act as an 'aide memoire' for the Bard himself.

 His views and comments on all these matters will be recorded for posterity and hopefully the question: Is SHAKESPEARE a pseudonym for other writers? Will be answered.

 Drummond G Marvin

Letter No. 11a - 11th April 2064

Dear Sir,

Shake --speare's Sonnets

Sonnets are often made up of a stanza of 8 lines (an octet) followed by six lines (a sestet) BUT in Shakespeare's/Marlowe's case the form is 3 sets of 4 lines followed by a couplet, embodying the statement and the resolution of a single theme.

Shakespeare/Marlowe wrote 154 sonnets. (Approx: 2,156 lines – give or take 3 or 4)

Marlowe coupled with Shakespeare's name is, in my opinion, the main contender for authorship of some of these sonnets, if not all. (Remember Abysmal) There are others suggested but not with the passion shown for Marlowe.
To be clear, I am not referring to the 'rival poet', talked of in sonnets 76-86 or 100-103, but only to the one assuming Shakespeare's identity and authorship, if indeed there was someone who did so.

It has been said that when published in 1609, by the unsavoury Thomas Thorpe (1580-1614), the sonnets were deliberately printed out of chronological order. Some had been taken from correspondence or manuscripts of other description and placed according to the editor's thinking.

These sonnets have been an enigma in terms of their meaning as well as to their relationship to the author's life and contemporary history – that is assuming the author to be William Shakespeare. There are strong arguments supporting not only Marlowe but others, including Edward de Vere, 17th Earl of Oxford, as being the wordsmith.

One of many assumptions shared by Scholars has been that the verses relate to real circumstances of the author's actual life. Having the correct author in place to find the correct life occurrences to match up with the verses will be paramount. With this end in view, and whilst still mainly supporting Shakespeare's entitlement as to authorship, I intend to present the Marlovian's claim as I believe Shakespeare has a case to answer. (Abysmal thinking no doubt).

If you are encouraged by what you are about to read, be warned that further research may prove fruitless; the paradox, 'did the Bard of Avon write all/some or none of the sonnets', is not likely to be solved.

11b - 11th April 2064
TIME LINE - 1542 -1616

William Shakespeare (1564 – 1616)
Christopher Marlowe   (1564 – 1593)
Queen Elizabeth I (1533 – 1603)

1542
Mary Queen of Scots crowned. She was next in line for the English throne after Henry VIII children (Edward, Mary and Elizabeth).

1547
Henry VIII died on 28th January. His son Edward was only 9 years of age and too young to rule.

1548
Edward's uncle, Edward Seymour, Duke of Somerset, was given the title Lord Protector. He ensured Edward VI was educated as a protestant.
William Cecil became his secretary.
The change over from growing crops to sheep farming caused wide-spread rioting as farmers were enclosing their lands which at one time had been common ground.
Some of the rioters demonstrated against Seymour's religious programme.

1549

Seymour urged compassion and on 14th June persuaded Edward VI to pardon all those that tore down fences and hedges. The gentry blamed Seymour for the unrest and encouraging the revolution. His main opponents included: John Dudley, 2nd Earl of Warwick, Henry Wriothesley, 2nd Earl of Southampton, Henry Howard, 1st Earl of Northampton, Nicholas Wotton and Ralph Sadler.

Seymour gave up his post and was deprived of all positions.

Cecil was arrested in November and imprisoned in the Tower of London.

1550

On 1st January William Cecil was released on the orders of John Dudley.

He was sworn in as one of two Secretaries of State for King Edward.

In September he was a member of the Privy Council.

1551

William Cecil became chancellor of the Order of the Garter (Losing his Secretary of State office).

William Cecil knighted. Although he had adopted Catholicism he was in correspondence with the young Elizabeth who invited him to become her estate manager.

In October John Dudley was granted the title Duke of Northumberland.

1553

On 6th July Edward VI died and the Duke of Northumberland attempted to take power by placing Lady Jane Grey on the throne. Mary Tudor fled to Norfolk and later to Framlingham in Suffolk. Cecil had initially supported Northumberland and had been forced to sign the document changing the order of succession (cutting out Mary and Elizabeth in favour of Lady Jane) but he made sure he had witnesses to his misgivings about signing. He decided to support Mary.

Dudley's troops deserted him and on 23rd July at Cambridge he surrendered and was imprisoned two days later, with his sons and friends, in the Tower.

He was tried for High Treason on 18th August and Mary had him executed at Tower Hill on 22nd August. In his final speech he warned the crowd to remain loyal to the Catholic Church.

William Cecil declined offers to serve in Mary's government. He was unwilling to be the executor of Catholic policy.

William Cecil elected to Parliament as knight of the shire of Lincolnshire. Also so elected in years 1555 and 1559.

1554

William Cecil agreed to go to Italy and bring Cardinal Reginald Pole to England.

1557
Shakespeare's father John aged 26 marries Mary Arden aged 17. John is elected ale-taster of the borough of Stratford.

1558
In the summer Mary had stomach pains which turned out to be cancer. She had to consider naming Elizabeth as her successor. She postponed naming her half-sister until the last moment on 6th November.
On 17th November Mary died, aged forty-two.
On Elizabeth's accession to the throne she appointed Sir William Cecil, who was thirty-eight, as her Chief Secretary of State. They both saw the nation's future as bound up with the Protestant Reformation.
He was also appointed as leader of Elizabeth's Privy Council and being concerned that Queen Elizabeth may be overthrown he provided money to Francis Walsingham to set-up Britain's first counter-intelligence network.
Walsingham was given responsibility for the security of the monarch. He created a network of spies in Europe. He received regular reports from: twelve locations in France, nine in Germany, four in Italy, four in Spain and three others in Europe.
He had informants in Constantinople, Algiers and Tripoli,
Although Cecil was a Protestant he was not a purist. He aided the Protestant Huguenots and

Dutch enough to ward off any dangers to England's shores.

1559
In February Sir William Cecil was elected Chancellor of Cambridge University. He intervened in Scotland and his share in the religious settlement was considerable. He grew more Protestant as time wore on. He was happier to persecute Catholics than Puritans. He had no love for ecclesiastical jurisdiction. (See entry year 1583).

1560
Robert Dudley, Earl of Leicester, emerged as one of Elizabeth's leading advisers and given the post of Master of the Horse. He was allotted official quarters in the palace. It became apparent she preferred Dudley's company to anyone else's.

Elizabeth gave Dudley land in Yorkshire as well as the manor of Kew. The story that the couple were lovers and Elizabeth was pregnant spread across the country.

In June a sixty-eight year old woman was arrested for saying that Elizabeth was pregnant by Robert Dudley.

John de Vere, the 16th Earl of Oxford wrote to Cecil with news that the vicar of Little Burstead had been detained for telling another man that the Queen "was with child". Oxford wanted to know if he should follow the usual punishment for "rumour-mongers" and cut of the vicar's ears.

1561

William Cecil given the lucrative office of Master of the Court of Wards and Liveries. As master he supervised the raising and education of wealthy aristocratic boys whose fathers had died before they had reached maturity. These included Edward de Vere, 17th Earl of Oxford, Henry Wriothesley, 3rd Earl of Southampton, and Roger Manners, 5th Earl of Rutland.

Thomas Walsingham, 1st Cousin (once removed) to Sir Francis Walsingham was born.

1563

Robert Cecil was born. (His elder brother was Thomas the Earl of Exeter and 2nd Baron, Burghley).

William Cecil was appointed Knight of the Shire of Northamptonshire.

1564

Christopher MARLOWE (hereinafter CM), born on 6th February and baptised 26th February at St George's Canterbury.

Father named 'John' a Shoemaker. Either family well off or connected as Marlowe was educated at the 'King's School' and at Cambridge.

William SHAKESPEARE (hereinafter WS), born 23 April (St George's Day) Father named 'John' a Glover and Wool Dealer. Free education owing to his father's civic status. Attended Stratford Grammar School renowned for the teaching of the Greek and Latin poets.

Sir William Cecil created MA at Cambridge University during Queen Elizabeth's visit there.

Thomas Drury (8 May 1551 – 26 August 1603) went up to Caius College, Cambridge as a Gentleman Pensioner. There is no record of his obtaining a degree, possibly because as a Catholic he refused to take the Protestant oath.

1565
John (Shakespeare's father) became an Alderman.

1566
Robert Devereux was born. (Destined to be 2nd Earl of Essex).

1567
The Red Lion Playhouse was opened.

1568
Mary Queen of Scots was imprisoned by Queen Elizabeth after the long term instigation of Sir William Cecil.

John Shakespeare became Bailiff of Stratford. (Mayor)

1569
Walsingham became suspicious of Roberto di Ridolfi, an Italian banker living in London. He brought him in for questioning.

1570

Ridolfi was released but some believed him to have been turned into a double agent for Walsingham. He (Rodolfi) attempted to develop close relationships with John Leslie, Bishop of Ross and Thomas Howard, 4th Duke of Norfolk, a cousin to the Queen and the highest ranking peer in England.

The Pope declared Queen Elizabeth to be illegitimate and released her subjects from obedience. This caused many plots to kill her but all were defeated by her secret service.

John Shakespeare became Chief Alderman. He was later accused in the Exchequer Court of Usury for lending money at the rate of 20% and 25% interest. His application to bear a Coat-of-Arms and for the title of 'gentleman' was refused

Thomas Drury's brother, William, married Sir Edward Stafford's sister Elizabeth.

1571

Sir William Cecil was created 1st Baron Burghley. He continued to act as Secretary of State.

Mary Queen of Scots wrote to the Duke of Norfolk on 31st January encouraging him to join the plot against Elizabeth. She suggested marriage. Norfolk did not lend his support but reluctantly agreed to meet Ridolfi which resulted in Norfolk giving verbal approval to the request for Spanish military assistance.

On 12th April, Charles Bailly, a servant of the Bishop of Ross, was arrested on his arrival at Dover. He was carrying banned books as well as ciphered correspondence about the plot between the Duke of Norfolk and his brother-in-law, John Lumley. Bailly was taken to the tower and tortured. This led to the arrest of the Bishop of Ross and the Duke of Norfolk.

Walsingham also arrested two of Norfolk's secretaries who had been carrying £600 in gold to Mary's Scottish supporters. Information under torture revealed nineteen letters to Norfolk from the Queen of Scots and the Bishop of Ross, hidden in the roof of one of Norfolk's houses.

On 7th September Norfolk was taken to the Tower of London.

1572

Sir Francis Walsingham appointed ambassador to France. His residence in Paris was used as a protestant refuge during St Bartholomew's Day Massacre. He did not enjoy a good relationship with the Queen.

Lord Burghley was appointed as Lord Treasurer. His main work as Secretary of State was carried out by his old friend Francis Walsingham.

On 16th January the Duke of Norfolk was brought to trial at Westminster Hall. He was convicted of High Treason, condemned to death and returned to the Tower

Elizabeth was reluctant to authorise the execution of the Duke of Norfolk. Warrants were repeatedly signed and then cancelled. William Cecil complained to Francis Walsingham "The Queens majesty hath always been a merciful lady and by mercy she hath taken more harm than by justice, and yet she thinks she is more beloved in doing herself harm."

On 19th April the Treaty of Blois was signed.

Elizabeth finally yielded to Parliament and although refusing to take action against Mary Queen of Scots agreed that Norfolk would be executed. She hoped to spare a fellow Queen.

On 2nd June the Duke of Norfolk was executed on Tower Hill.

1573
On 6 October, Henry Wriothesley was born. (Son of 2nd Earl of Southampton).

Charles Howard, a cousin of Queen Elizabeth, succeeded to the titles of 1st Earl of Nottingham and 2nd Baron Howard of Effingham.

1576
Robert Devereux succeeded his father to the title 2nd Earl of Essex.

1577

The Newington Butts Playhouse and Curtain Theatres opened.

1578

John Shakespeare fell behind with his taxes.

1579

John Shakespeare is forced to mortgage Asbies from Mary Arden's estate.

1580

CM, on 10 December, obtained an Archbishop Parker Scholarship from All Kings School, Canterbury to Corpus Christie College, Cambridge.

Earl of Oxford was accused of urging Thomas Drury to kill the Earl of Arundel

Thomas Walsingham was appointed by Sir Francis as a trusted courier between the English court and the queen's ambassador in France.
JS is fined £40 for missing a court date.

1581

On 4 October Henry Wriothesley inherited the title of 3rd Earl of Southampton. He landed an income of £1,097.6s per annum. The Queen sold his wardship and marriage to Lord Howard of Effingham for £1,000 and Howard entered into some form of agreement with Lord Burghley transferring the custody and marriage of the young Earl but left Howard holding his lands.

Thomas accompanied Sir Francis to Paris on a delicate diplomatic mission concerning the proposed marriage between Elizabeth and the French King's brother, Francis, Duke of Anjou.

On 21 September a Richard Baines was ordained as a priest working undercover for Sir Francis Walsingham.

1582

On 28th May Richard Baines was unmasked as a spy when he tried to poison Dr William Allen, founder and President of Rheims Catholic College. He was imprisoned for a year and was released only when he signed a confession.

Henry Wriothesley, aged 8, went to live in Cecil House, The Strand.

WS aged 18 married Anne Hathaway, aged 26, of Shottery, who gave birth to Susanna, 6 months after wedding.

1583

Sir Edward Stafford appointed English Ambassador in Paris.

CM translated Ovid's Amores which was published in 1596 and First Book of Lucan's Pharsalia published in 1600. (POEMS)

On 10 March the Queen's Company was formed.

In April Sir Francis Walsingham received a report from Henry Fagot, one of his agents inside the French Embassy, that a Francis Throckmorton, one of England's most promising Catholics, had dined with the ambassador.
On 13th May, Baines was released from prison.
William Cecil warmly remonstrated with John Whitgift, the Anglican Archbishop of Canterbury, over his persecuting articles.
In November Walsingham ordered the arrest of Throckmorton in his London home. On the rack he admitted the plot against Elizabeth and implicated the Spanish ambassador.

1584
CM graduated from Cambridge with a BA degree.

Robert Cecil entered parliament.

Henry Fagot wrote again to Sir Francis Walsingham stating that "the chief agents for the Queen of Scots are Throckmorton and Lord Henry Howard."

On 10th July Francis Throckmorton was executed at Tyburn.

Thomas Walsingham given a trusted position in the state's intelligence operation against Catholic plots. He operated from his own office in Sir Francis's house in Seething Lane, next door to the Tower.

1585
The Treaty of Nonsuch was signed by Elizabeth of England and the Dutch Republic.

The Earl of Essex served in the Netherlands until 1586.

Earl of Nottingham was appointed Lord High Admiral and served as commissioner at the trial of Mary Queen of Scots.

Twins Hamnet and Judith Shakespeare born.

WS finished with his education and joined one of the many touring companies of players. Actors were held in low esteem by the general public; unless of course patronage was procured. He remained in Stratford until he was 25.

For some unknown reason Thomas Drury was in Fleet prison until 22 June.

The spelling of CM's family name was fluid. CM appears as: 'Marlowe'; Marlow; 'Marle' and 'Marley' (which is the only known signature) At university he was known as 'Marlin' or 'Merlin' and 'Kit' has been mentioned. He was referred to as 'Morley' in the Coroner's Inquest.

In October the Earl of Southampton, aged 12, was admitted to St John's College, Cambridge.

1585/6
Aged 21 CM started but did not complete - The Tragedy of Dido, Queen of Carthage (PLAY)

1586
John Shakespeare was removed from the Board of Aldermen.

On 17th July Robert Poley, Sir Francis Walsingham's agent, trapped Anthony Babington resulting in Mary Queen of Scots being tried and sentenced to death. On 29th September at Fothering Hay Castle Mary Queen of Scots was executed. (Beheaded) (n.b. in 1612 King James 1 of England (her son) had her exhumed and transferred to the Henry V11 Chapel, at Westminster Abbey).

On 15th October Sir John Puckering elected to Parliament as Speaker. He was involved in deciding the fate of Mary Queen of the Scots.

1587
CM was refused (initially) an MA degree as he was a suspected Roman Catholic. However advisers to H.M.Queen Elizabeth 1 recommended that he should receive it. Mention was made of his (CM's) services to the State. Rumour has it that he was a spy for the Queen.

CM's production of Tamburlaine the Great (parts 1 & 2) (PLAY – 18,751 & 19,317) was performed by the Admiral's Men with Edward Alleyn in the lead.

The Earl of Essex was appointed Master of the Horse.

In December The Lord Chamberlain's Men Troupe was formed. The Rose theatre was built.

Thomas Drury was described as Sir Edward Stafford's iniquitous secretary in Paris.

1588

Earl of Nottingham appointed Commander in Chief of the British Navy.

Spanish Armada defeated.

CM The Tragical History of Doctor Faustus. (PLAY – 12,802)

1589

Aged 25 years WS left Stratford for London where he prospered as actor (we know of the Ghost in Hamlet) / playwright / Poet. But he continued to own his house in Stratford and bought more properties there.

On 6th June The Earl of Southampton graduated from Cambridge with a degree.

On 6th October the Earl of Southampton was 16 years of age as noted by Lord Burghley in his diary.

In November, on the death of his older brother Edmund, Thomas Walsingham inherited the manor of Scadbury, Kent. His debts had been mounting.

On 18th September, in Hog Lane, Bishopsgate a Tom Watson, a writer and friend of CM's, killed

William Bradley in a duel. CM was present and both were arrested. CM spent 12 days in Newgate Prison and on 3rd December Watson was acquitted having pleaded self-defence.
WS's Comedy of Errors (PLAY – 14,701)
CM's the Jew of Malta. (PLAY – 20,545)

1590
Thomas Walsingham spent some time in Fleet Debtors prison before taking up residence at Scadbury Manor. He employed Ingram Frizer as his business agent, advancing money to needy heirs against the security of their inheritance. Thomas came into his own inheritance.
Earl of Essex underwent a clandestine marriage to Frances Walsingham (Daughter of Sir Francis).
Lord Burghley was negotiating with the Earl of Southampton's grandfather, Anthony Browne, 1st Viscount Montgomery, and Southampton's mother, Mary Countess of Wriothesley (1552 – 1607), for a marriage between Southampton and Lord Burghley's eldest grand-daughter, Elizabeth Vere, daughter of Burghley's daughter, Anne Cecil, and Edward de Vere, 17th Earl of Oxford.
The match was not to Southampton's liking and rumour has it he had to pay £5,000.00 to be released.
CM's Tamburlaine the Great (parts 1 & 2) Published.
WS's Henry VI (part 2) and Henry VI (part 3). (PLAYS – 25,439 and 24,294)
(CM may have assisted in the writing.)

1591

WS's Henry VI (part 1) (PLAY – 21,607) CM may have assisted.

Robert Persons, a Catholic priest, published Responsio. It included an attack on Lord Burghley's view on religion, describing him as a "malignant worm" and "ambitious serpent", and accused him not only of atheism but of opening the way to atheist teaching in the universities.

Responsio also included an attack on Sir Walter Raleigh described as the leader of a group of thinkers whose passion was to explore the world and the mind. The group included, among others, the writers: Christopher Marlowe, Thomas Kyd, George Chapman and Matthew Roydon. The men would either meet at the homes of Raleigh, Edward de Vere, 17th Earl of Oxford, or Henry Percy, 9th Earl of Northumberland.

Lord Burghley was concerned when Raleigh became Captain of the Guard. He disliked Raleigh and plotted to have him removed from power. He discovered Raleigh was having an affair with Elizabeth 'Bess' Throckmorton, one of the Queen's Gentlewoman of the Privy Chamber.

Earl of Essex commanded the forces sent to help Henry IV of France against the Catholic league.

On 13th May, six months after Sir Edward's recall, a warrant was issued and Drury was arrested at his home. His premises were searched for 'matters of State'.

On 15th May Drury was taken to Marshalsea prison charged with 'divers great and fond matters' and spent the next two years there. He had been informed on and arrested by his companion Richard Cholmeley who was employed by Robert Cecil and the Privy Council as an anti-Catholic agent. Cholmeley maintained he was involved in the 'apprehension of Papists and other dangerous men'. Cholmeley was described as a pseudo-Catholic using his origin and connections to entrap Catholics.

Robert Cecil appointed to the Privy Council. Other members: Archbishop of Canterbury (Whitgift); Lord Keeper (PUCKERING); Lord Treasurer (Burghley); Lord Derby; Lord Chamberlain (Hunsden); Lord Buckhurst; Sir John Wolley; and Sir John Fortesque. (NOT PRESENT: Lord Admiral (Howard) and The Earl of Essex.)

In July Bess Throckmorton discovered she was pregnant.

On 19th November Raleigh married Bess in secret and she kept up the subterfuge, by disguising her pregnancy at court. She waited until the last minute before leaving court knowing that if she could be away for less than a fortnight she would not need a licence.

1592

The Great Plague closed Theatres. Shakespeare wrote poems and started to write his 154 sonnets.

On 29th March Bess gave birth to a son, Damerei. Soon after she was back in the Queen's service as though nothing had happened.

Lord Burghley arranged for his twenty seven year old son, Robert Cecil, to carry out an investigation, having been made aware of the rumours at court.

In May Burghley took the evidence gained to Elizabeth and both were placed under house arrest.

In August Bess and Raleigh were sent to the Tower.

In October their son, Damerei, died from the plague.

WS's Richard III. (PLAY – 29,278)

CM's The Tragedy of Edward ii. (PLAY)

CM was deported from Vissingen on a counterfeiting charge.

In October Viscount Montague died.

In the autumn Thomas Drury was interviewed about what Cholmeley had told him about figures such as Christopher Marlowe, Francis Drake, Walter Raleigh, Charles Howard and William Cecil. Apparently Marlowe had told Cholmeley he had read the atheist lecture to Raleigh and others.

On 8th November Lord Buckhurst wrote to his fellow Privy Councillor Lord Keeper Puckering telling him he had visited Drury as Puckering had requested him to do. Buckhurst's assessment was that if Drury may have liberty and leave to go beyond the seas he will adventure himself somewhat to do some service.

On 25th December John Shakespeare was fined for missing church.

1593

CM's The Massacre at Paris. (PLAY – 11,084) CM's Hero and Leander. (POEM) The poem was written at Sir Thomas Walsingham's estate at Scadbury Manor, Kent.

WS's Venus and Adonis 18 April 1593 (POEM) Published after CM's death. It has been suggested that it was written by CM under an assumed name of WS. It included the phrase 'first heir of my invention' in the dedication to the Earl of Southampton as well as some lines from the Ovidian poem previously translated by CM.

In March Sir Walter Raleigh upset Queen Elizabeth and her Privy Council by making a speech in the House of Commons against proposed legislation to enforce religious conformity aimed at both Catholic and Puritan dissenters.

On 20 March Richard Cholmeley was arrested for Heresy and confessed he'd been converted to "atheism" by Marlowe.

On 5th May a libellous verse appeared on the wall of a Dutch church in Broad Street signed by 'Tamburlaine' and refers to other CM plays.

John Penry, a Welsh puritan martyr, was arrested for writing, treasonable, subversive literature. He was sentenced to die on 25th May but his execution at the gallows was delayed until 29th May.

By May 1593 Drury appeared to be doing some service for Puckering. Anti-immigrant posters had been appearing in London, one of the most vicious being the so-called 'Dutch Church Libel' which was posted on 5th May. It was written in blank verse and signed Tamberlaine. It contained references to two other plays of Christopher Marlowe's. Thomas Drury was sent to stay with Richard Baines, an acquaintance of his, as it was believed he knew who was responsible.

On 10th May the Lord Mayor offered 100 crowns reward for information, and the following day the Privy Council authorised torture in discovering the perpetrator.

On 12th May the playwright Thomas Kyd had been arrested and in his chamber was found fragments of what were called 'vile heretical conceits denying the deity of Jesus Christ our saviour'. Kyd claimed they were Marlowe's who had shared a room with him. Under torture at Bridewell prison Kyd made a series of allegations concerning Marlowe's atheism which he confirmed in writing to Puckering.

Thomas Drury was preparing his own list of accusations, the so-called 'Remembrances' against Richard Cholmeley and his 'damnable crew'. He alleged they used Marlowe as their guru claiming he was 'able to show more sound reasons for atheism than any Divine in England is able to give to prove divinity'.

Drury claimed he had instigated the production of the 'Baines' Note' and had delivered it to. After spending two years in prison because of Cholmeley's treachery and knowing that Baines and Marlowe had 'malice one to another' it follows there was some collusion between Drury and Baines to bring about the demise of both Marlowe and Cholmeley.

On 18 May an arrest warrant was issued for CM with no reason given. CM had recently written an heretical manuscript and blasphemy was suspected. This charge was punishable by being boiled alive, hanged drawn and quartered or burnt on the stake.

On 20 May CM was arrested and bailed on condition he reported daily to the Privy Council at the Star Chamber Court. Soon after his arrest Richard Baines, an old enemy of CM's produced his note to the Privy Council saying that CM had scorned the scriptures and the church. He was also involved in 'coining'. He further maintained that CM had read his atheist lecture to Sir Walter Raleigh and others. These allegations were all capital crimes. This note was similar to Baines' confession at the Catholic Seminary at Rheims in 1582.

On 29th May Penry was executed at St Thomas-a-Watering two miles from Deptford. He had written to Lord Burghley and the Earl of Essex hoping to have his sentence commuted. One of the many conspiracy theories suggests Burghley together with Robert Cecil arranged for Penry's body to taken to Deptford to double for Marlowe.

On 30 May CM was stabbed to death by Ingram Fritzer at the private victualing house of the widow, Dame Eleanor Bull. The death was alleged to have been as a result of a dispute as to who should pay the reckoning.

Those present were:

Ingram Fritzer, the personal servant and business agent of CM's patron – the wealthy Thomas Walsingham, cousin of the recently deceased Sir Francis Walsingham, creator of the espionage service. Thomas himself was a master spy. On 28 June, after only four weeks in custody Fritzer was granted a pardon by Queen Elizabeth.

Robert Poley an experienced government agent who carried the Queens most important correspondence to and from the courts in Europe. It is said that he had arrived at Deptford from The Hague where he'd been on the Queen's business.

Nicholas Skeres, seemingly a minor cog in Walsingham's spy machine. At this time he was involved with Fritzer in a project to fleece a naïve young man of his money. (Conny catching).

Christopher Marlowe enjoyed both the friendship and patronage of Thomas Walsingham and at the time of his arrest was staying at Walsingham's estate at Scadbury in Kent. He had gone there to escape the plague in London.

Thomas Walsingham was a mourner at Marlowe's funeral.

WS's Taming of the Shrew and Titus Andronicus (PLAYS – 21,055 and 20,743)

Lord Keeper Puckering interrogated John Whitfield, a Catholic recusant involved with Francis Dacre in a plot for a Spanish invasion of Scotland.

On 28th June Cholmeley was arrested and tortured to reveal other 60 members of the sect in his group. The 'sect' turned out to be just four men all of whom had at one time been government spies or turncoat Catholics. At the end of May Cholmeley was imprisoned and never heard of again.

1594

Plague over and Theatres opened. WS joined The Lord Chamberlain's Men, a touring company, playing in Stratford, for which he wrote several plays. He was entitled to a share in the profits. Actors included Richard Burbage, Edward Alleyn, and Will Kempe. The company performed at the Court of Queen Elizabeth during the Christmas festivities 1594/95.

WS The Two Gentlemen of Verona. (PLAY 17,129)

WS Rape of Lucrece 9th May 1594.(Dedicated to the Earl of Southampton couched in extravagant terms "The love I dedicate to your Lordship is without end..." He continues saying that what he has done and what he is about to do is Southampton's. (POEM)
WS Romeo and Juliet (24,545), Two Gentlemen of Verona (17,129) and Love's Labour's Lost. (21,459 - PLAYS)

1595
WS Richard II and Midsummer Night's Dream (PLAYS – 22,423 & 16,511)
19th October 1595 Philip Howard, 20th Earl of Arundel died of dysentery in the Tower of London having been imprisoned there in 1985 (25th April) on charges of high treason which were never proven. Anne Dacre was left as his widow.

1596
Lord Puckering died of apoplexy.
On 28th June Sir Francis Drake dies of the plague whilst at sea.
WS's son Hamnet died aged 11 years.
Earl of Nottingham and Earl of Essex took part in the capture of Cadiz.
Thomas Walsingham appointed Justice of the Peace for the Kent Hundreds, Earl of Essex of Rokersley. He organised the defences against the Armada and was knighted shortly afterwards.
WS King John and The Merchant of Venice, (PLAYS – 20,772 & 21,291)

In October of this year WS's father, John, was awarded a grant of arms which entitled him to be referred to as 'gentleman'. WS finances heavily supported his father.

Robert Cecil appointed Elizabeth's Secretary of State.

WS Henry IV (parts 1 & 2) Merry Wives of Windsor (PLAYS 24,579, 25 ,689 & 21,845)

1597

WS bought in May, 'New Place', the 2nd largest house in Stratford on Avon for £60.00.

Earl of Essex was appointed Earl Marshall and was responsible for the failure of the expedition to the Azores.

The Earl of Southampton courted Mistress Vernon, Queen Elizabeth's maid of honour. Elizabeth was not pleased.

1598

Thomas Walsingham knighted.

Sir William Cecil, 1st Baron Burghley & Queen Elizabeth's Lord High Treasurer died.

On 17th March Earl of Southampton offered his military services to Henry IV in France. The campaign ended with the peace of Vervius and Southampton returned to England after a stay in Paris of several months and married mistress Vernon.

WS mentioned as among the chief holders of corn and malt in Stratford.

WS and other company members financed the building of the Globe Theatre.

WS Henry V & Much Ado about Nothing. (PLAYS – 26,119 & 21,157)
WS Passionate Pilgrim. (POEM)

1599
Earl of Essex quarrelled with Queen Elizabeth as a result of turning his back on her when retiring. She boxed his ears and they were never reconciled. The Earl served 6 months Lieutenancy of Ireland which failed and he was returned to England and imprisoned.
Chamberlain's men build the Globe Theatre at Bankside on the South Bank of the Thames. WS achieved success with Henry V, Julius Caesar & Twelfth Night.
WS Twelfth Night;; As You Like It and Julius Caesar. (PLAYS – 19,837; 21,690 & 19,703)

1600
WS Hamlet; and Merry Wives of Windsor (PLAYS – 30,557 & 21,845) Richard Burbage took the role of Hamlet & WS played the Ghost.

1601
Earl of Essex and Earl of Southampton plotted to raise revolt in London to remove Elizabeth's councillors. They sought to influence the public to join them by exhibiting at the Globe Theatre and other places in London a play on the subject of Richard II. It was about the deposing and killing of Richard II. WS's play of the same name had been printed in 1597 with the suppression of 154 lines containing the trial and the deposing of

the King. Elizabeth feared this deposing exhibition in the 'old' Richard II play would stir up the people against her.

On 19th February both Earls were charged and found guilty of High Treason. The Earl of Oxford was on Jury service and Essex was beheaded. The Earl of Nottingham had quelled the rebellion.

WS Troilus and Cressida. (PLAY – 26,089).

WS's acting group The Lord Chamberlain's Men were commissioned to stage Richard II at the Globe Theatre.

8th September John Shakespeare, (died nearly 70 years old,) is buried.

1602

Lord Puckering's widow, Jane (nee Chowne) married William Combe, who with his nephew John Combe, sold land in Stratford to WS.

WS All's Well That Ends Well. (PLAY – 23,009).

WS on 1st May buys land in Stratford for £320.00.

1603

Thomas Drury died of the Bubonic Plague in his lodgings at the Swan Inn, Southwark.

On 24th March Queen Elizabeth I died.

On 7th May Edward de Vere, 17th Earl of Oxford, wrote to Secretary of State Robert Cecil as follows:

"But I hope truth is subject to no prescription, for truth is truth though never so old, and time cannot make that false which was once true."

Cecil had forced Oxford to sacrifice his identity, both as the father of the Queen's heir and as the author of the 'Shakespeare' works dedicated publicly to Southampton, who had to renounce his claim of succession in return for his life and freedom and royal pardon.

Henry Wriothesley, 3rd Earl of Southampton was released from the Tower.

1604

Edward de Vere, 17th Earl of Oxford died.

Robert Cecil negotiated the peace terms with Spain.

WS Othello & Measure for Measure. (PLAYS – 26,450 & 21,780)

1605

Robert Cecil rewarded with an Earldom by James 1 and took the title 1st Earl of Salisbury.

WS King Lear & Macbeth. (16,145 & 17,121)

1606

WS & Timon of Athens (PLAY –, & 18,216)

WS Phoenix and the Turtle (POEM)

1607

WS Pericles (PLAY - 18,529)

1608

Earl of Salisbury (Robert Cecil) appointed Lord Treasurer. He was fighting a losing battle against Royal debts.

WS Anthony and Cleopatra; and Coriolanus; (PLAYS – 24,905 & 27,589)
WS becomes part owner with the King's Men of Blackfriars Theatre.

1609

Thomas Thorpe published Shakespeare's sonnets without his permission.
WS Cymbeline and The Winter's Tale. (PLAYS – 27,565 & 24,914)
WS Lover's Complaint. (POEM)

1610

WS Tempest. (PLAY – 16,633)

1611

WS (Together with John Fletcher) The Two Noble Kinsmen. (PLAY – 25,424)

1612

WS (With Fletcher) Henry VIII (PLAY – 24,629)

1613

WS (With Fletcher) Cardenio. (PLAY – Unknown)
In May WS's company, The King's Men, were paid to perform six plays amongst which was Cardenio. They also received a large sum of money to perform this before the ambassador of the Duke of Savoy.
Later in the century a London printer registered Cardenio for publication and listed the play's authors as WS and John Fletcher

June 29th the Globe was destroyed by fire.

1614
Sir Thomas Walsingham was returned to Parliament as Knight of the shire of Kent.
The Globe Theatre was rebuilt.

1616
On 10th February, Judith, WS's daughter, marries Thomas Quiney, a Vintner in Stratford.
On 12th March Judith and Thomas Quiney were excommunicated for marrying without the Bishop's approval during the period of Lent.
On 25th March Shakespeare amends and signs his will.
He struck out his son-in-law, replacing him with Judith his daughter whom he bequeathed £100.00 (£20,000.00 by 2017's standards), in discharge of her marriage porcion, another £50.00 if she relinquished the Chapel Lane cottage also if she or her children were alive three years after the date of this will a further £150.00 would be available of which she would receive the interest but not the principal. Judith was also given 'my Broad Silver Gilt Bole'. Finally the bulk of WS's estate included: his main house New Place, two houses in Henley Street, and various lands in and around Stratford.

23rd April, Shakespeare's death

On 25th April he was buried in the Chancel of Holy Trinity Church in Stratford.

Letter No. 12 - 14 April 2064

Dear Sir,

Apparently I was chosen to lead this experiment, as the powers that be wanted an investigator and not an academic/scholar/archivist or the like. They didn't specify the degree of investigatory ability required, which is just as well. As a matter of fact I nearly didn't get the job. At the interview, having recently retired from the police force, I was asked what I knew about Will Shakespeare. I gave this some consideration and said "Give me five minutes and I'll soon get something on him." They thought that was my sense of humour and I got the job.

I must now declare my position regarding the question 'Did Shakespeare write his own work or, was his name used as a pseudonym and assumed by another?' Saying that Shakespeare didn't write his own work is like saying there is no Santa Claus! It's like Hamlet without the prince. Of course he wrote his own stuff…or so I thought until, I read up on Christopher Marlowe. Could it have been him all along?

I don't really have answers but I may have certain lines of enquiry that either you the reader or any archivist could possibly solve. I will shortly deal with my observations about Shakespeare himself, followed with those of Marlowe. I would, however, like to map out, again in the form of a short history lesson, this particular period (1558 – 1593) and some of the characters involved.

In 1558 Queen Elizabeth 1st acceded to the throne of England appointing Sir William Cecil as her Chief Secretary of State and leader of her Privy Council. Although now a Protestant he was not a purist. He was happier persecuting Catholics than Puritans. He had no love for ecclesiastical jurisdiction. In 1559 he was elected Chancellor of Cambridge University.
Cecil aided the Huguenots and Dutch enough to ward off any danger to England's shores. He became the creator of Elizabeth's intelligence service under the direction of Sir Francis Walsingham. (Later, Cecil's son Robert would also be involved).

On 6 February 1564 Christopher Marlowe was born. He received an excellent education attending King's School, Canterbury and later graduated from Cambridge. (N.B. at this time there were only two Universities in England – Oxford and Cambridge.)

On 23 April 1564 William Shakespeare was born. His father was a 'Glover' and 'Wool Dealer'. Owing to his father's civic status his son received a free education. He attended Stratford Grammar School renowned for the teachings of

Greek and Latin poets. He did not progress to University. He in fact joined and stayed with a band of touring players, who were using Stratford upon Avon as their base.

In 1571 Sir William Cecil was created 1st Baron Burghley.
It is not necessary, at this stage, to go into too much detail in telling this particular story. Suffice it to say in 1580 Marlowe obtained a scholarship to Corpus Christie College, Cambridge where in 1582 he translated, from the Greek, Ovid's Amores and the First Book of Lucan's Pharsalia. He graduated in 1584 with a BA degree; he was refused an MA, as he was suspected of being a Roman Catholic. However in 1587 advisers to Queen Elizabeth recommended he should receive it for services to the state. Rumour had it he was a spy.

Shakespeare, at the age of 18, married Anne Hathaway, who was 8 years older and pregnant. Their daughter Susanna was born six months after the wedding. It would seem that although Shakespeare had joined the cast of a touring company, presently based in Stratford, he became involved in real estate as well. It is not known, I believe, how this was financed.

Continued in letter 12a

Drummond G Marvin

Letter No. 12a - 14 April 2064

Dear Sir,

In 1587 Marlowe's production of Tamburlaine the Great was performed by the Admiral's Men with Edward Alleyn in the lead. Alleyn was a renowned actor of the time and his involvement supports those who hold Marlowe in high esteem. Critics considered Marlowe to be the father of English tragedy and blank verse. In fact Shakespeare paid tribute to him in "As you like it" (1599) by quoting some lines from Marlowe's poem "Hero and Leander".

In 1589 Shakespeare left Stratford for London where he prospered as an actor/playwright/poet. It must be said that actors/minstrels/performers were not highly regarded and struggled, without a patron's support.
Patrons could be found amongst the nobility who used actors/theatres/touring groups of players etc to enhance their social status. Their livery would be on display and their identity and good deeds advertised.

Shakespeare obtained the patronage of Queen Elizabeth and some others – one of whom was 16 year old, Henry Wriothesley, the 3rd Earl of Southampton. This young man figures in

Shakespeare's sonnets or so it is believed. More of this later.

Getting back to the main story, at this time (1589) Marlowe was involved when his friend Tom Watson killed another man in a duel. Both were arrested and imprisoned but soon released having their evidence of self-defence believed. I mention this to support those who say Marlowe's character is not to be admired; he has been imprisoned in Holland for counterfeiting and suspected of acts of heresy. He mixed with characters of ill repute.

Mention must be made of another who plays an important part, at this time (1589), in the main story. Thomas Walsingham, 1st cousin to Sir Francis Walsingham (deceased), inherited the manor at Scadbury Kent. Thomas's debts had put him in Fleet debtor's prison. When released he employed an Ingram Frizer as his business agent. This man killed Marlowe.
Whichever way you look at it, this now could be the beginning of the end or the ending of the beginning of this story. To begin or not to begin, that is the question...does that remind you of something?

On 5th May 1593 a libellous verse signed 'Tamburlaine' was revealed on the wall of a Dutch Church in London. John Penry, a Welsh puritan martyr was arrested and sentenced to die on 25th May. Penry had written to Lord

Burleigh (William Cecil) in an unsuccessful attempt to get his sentence commuted.

Thomas Kyd, playwright and friend, was arrested and under torture implicated Marlowe in treasonable acts of heresy and atheism. Prior to this a Richard Cholmeley had been in custody and had also implicated Marlowe in his conversion to atheism. Things were stacking up until finally Richard Baines, a professional spy, filed a lengthy document with the Privy Council impeaching Marlowe as a heretic.

On 18th May 1593 an arrest warrant was issued as blasphemy was suspected. This was a charge punishable by either being boiled alive, hanged drawn and quartered or burnt at the stake. On 20th May Marlowe was arrested and bailed! He was required to report daily to the Star Chamber.

The 25th May passed and Penry's execution was put on hold. Either William or his son Robert delayed the execution until 29th May, when his hanging was finally carried out.

On 30th May, Marlowe and three others, including Ingram Frizer, met up at a private victualing house in Deptford Kent for dinner and supper. Either at supper time or shortly afterwards, an argument between Marlowe and Frizer ended when Marlowe was stabbed to death. It would seem the disagreement was who should pay the bill – the reckoning.

Drummond G Marvin

Letter No. 13 - 16th April 2064

Dear Sir,

Outline of the Marlovian Case

The story told by the sonnets has no connection to the life of Shakespeare but it has to that of Marlowe, following his dramatic subterfuge at Deptford. This of course supports the theory that Marlowe's 'death' was indeed faked. If you believe he was in fact killed in 1593 then that's an end to it. BUT if his death was faked then he could very well be the author of the sonnets and plays, or at least some of them.

Both poets (Shakespeare and Marlowe) were of the same age so how long did Marlowe's second 'life' last? He is suspected of writing the poem 'Venus and Adonis' that was published after his reported death under Shakespeare's name. This poem included a dedication to the Earl of Southampton which contained a phrase and lines from a work previously translated by Marlowe.

We see from the 'Time Line' following letter 11, that in 1611, prior to Shakespeare's death, he engaged the services of a John Fletcher, poet and playwright, and together they produced: 'The Two Noble Kinsmen', 'Henry V111' and

'Cardino.' Could this mean Marlowe was no longer available? Was his 'final' death about 1611 or just before? (ABYSMAL)

Mention must be made of Henry Wriothesley, 3rd Earl of Southampton, who figures throughout sonnets 1 – 126.
He is seemingly younger than the poet who is addressing him. The poems form together an anatomy of the shifting moods of love. At first the poet seems to urge this fellow to marry and breed (1 – 17). The friendship grows in intensity and enforced separation causes grief (27 – 32). Mention is made in further sonnets of the Earl as time and age progresses but for the purposes of establishing possible authorship I intend to refer only to two sonnets No's 34 and 74.

The facts to support these Marlovian theories are that on 18th May, 1593 an arrest warrant was drawn up for Christopher Marlowe, with no reason given.
On 20th May he was arrested and bailed to report daily to the Privy Council, who were temporarily housed in the Star Chamber's premises.
On 30th May Marlowe was stabbed to death (through his right eye) by one of Sir Thomas Walsingham's retainers, whilst arguing who should pay for the meal they had all consumed.
An inquest decided that Marlowe's attacker had acted in self-defence and shortly afterwards he (the accused) was pardoned.

SONNET 34

Why didst though promise such a beauteous day,
And make me travel forth without my cloak,
To let base clouds o'ertake me in my way,
Hiding thy bravery in their rotten smoke?
'Tis not enough that through the cloud thou break,
To dry the rain on my storm-beaten face,
For no man well of such a salve can speak,
That heals the wound, and cures not the disgrace:
Nor can thy shame give physic to my grief;
Though thou repent, yet I have still the loss:
The offender's sorrow lends but weak relief
To him that bears the strong offence's cross.
Ah! But those tears are pearl which thy love sheds,
And they are rich and ransom all ill deeds.

It is believed that this sonnet gives the general background for the faking of Marlowe's death. It is suggested to be the first sonnet written after the Deptford event and speaks of the disgrace Marlowe suffered, because of the way they had to script the story for the benefit of the Coroner; telling him the accused had been attacked by Marlowe from behind to ensure he would go free.

We are asked to presume that when Marlowe had been summoned to report daily to the Privy Council, Sir Thomas Walsingham, who was Marlowe's patron and host – as the poet had been staying with him to avoid the London plague – had devised a plan for Marlowe to avoid the death penalty.

Why didst thou promise such a beauteous day,

If Marlowe had indeed been killed, would Shakespeare have known promises had been made to be able to write this? Who told him? Certainly not Walsingham or the remaining gang of three. It would not be in anyone's interests to reveal what would amount to a treasonable plot.

Is there a different meaning to the line? Could he have said, Drink as much as you want to-day, for to-morrow you meet your maker. The day Marlowe was 'killed' was, by all indications, the day he had to finally report to the Privy Council; could that be described as beauteous?

If you want my Abysmal opinion I would suggest, apart from doing nothing there were only four options available.

1. Report to the Privy Council and plea your case.
2. Run-away/escape never to return
3. Fake your death and exile yourself
4. Commit suicide/allow yourself to be killed.

Sonnet 34, according to the scholars, tells us that Marlowe was not present at Deptford the day they faked his death. He didn't take part in framing the story. It would seem he was writing to Sir Thomas Walsingham whose employee (Ingram Fritzer) gave 'Marlowe' a mortal wound, in his right eye.

It is thought that when the beauteous remark was made Walsingham would have told Marlowe his death was to be faked and he would escape the barbaric ending anticipated. However plans had to be adjusted to allow for a legal report of the death to ward off further suspicion and bring in the verdict of self-defence. Lord Burghley, in league with Thomas Walsingham, is attributed with this change of direction.

And make me travel forth without my cloak

If Marlowe didn't go to Deptford and his faked death was staged then the placing of Marlowe's cloak on the body would be of evidential value, as to identity. Marlowe, as witnessed in his portraits, was heavily into the display of haute couture. Whilst at Cambridge he was renowned for his distinctive, expensive fashion accoutre. This was put down to his earnings as a spy.

There are schools of thought that believe this line refers to the English proverbial 'Although the sun shines leave not thy cloak at home'. I am at odds with this because he is not saying he has FORGOTTEN to leave his cloak but that he has been MADE TO LEAVE IT! I believe this could be read, 'And made me exiled/cast out without my cloak'.

Ed: note. This, of course, would ruin any 'beat', 'rhythm' or 'acrostic cryptogram' embedded in the previous verse structure.

To let base clouds o'ertake me in my way,
Hiding thy brav'ry in their rotten smoke?

I believe this is Marlowe acknowledging Thomas Walsingham's courageous decision to thwart John Whitgift, the Archbishop of Canterbury, and to some extent the Privy Council itself, from executing his protégée, friend and house-guest. There are those who translate 'thy brav'ry' to mean 'your radiance'.

Later, the writer continues with: '*dry the rain on my storm-beaten face*'.
Could this mean, in order to escape, Marlowe undertook a sea voyage from Deptford, on a three masted Carrack and having to travel steerage, as circumstances dictated?

Before leaving Sonnet 34 mention must be made of the suggestion that Lord Burghley assisted Walsingham's decision to give his retainer the 'Self Defence' option. If Marlowe was not present at Deptford then who was? I believe he was there during daylight hours but another took his place at night time. This would be supper time and candle-lit. Was this a living person later killed or was it a corpse collected from a cemetery or a jail nearby?

Looking at the TIME LINE a John Penry was arrested and sentenced to die on 25th May 1593. He wrote to Lord Burghley and the Earl of Essex, hoping to have his sentence commuted. His execution was delayed until 29th May, the day before the Deptford incident. Could his body have been used in faking Marlowe's 'death'? If so, then we may have answers to the questions as to: why were there four people on this day out? None was particularly friendly with any other. Why was Eleanor Bull's Victualing House chosen? Was it a safe house used by the intelligence community? What happened during the four or five hours after dinner and before supper?

We are told that Eleanor Bull was a cousin of Blanche Parry, who, not only was Queen Elizabeth's favourite nanny, but also a cousin of Lord Burghley. Thus Eleanor Bull would be a witness of repute running an establishment for gentlemen. If she had to give evidence she surely would be believed. William Danby, the Queen's coroner, should have been accompanied by the County Coroner at the inquest, but acted alone. Danby was great friends with Lord Burghley.

The possible answers could be that Marlowe (or the intended victim) and three others, had to arrive at the venue. One of the three would be selected as the 'killer', the other two would be required to give false evidence to support the story of self-defence. During the lengthy interval between meals (4 to 5 hours) their claims to have been in the large garden were neither challenged nor corroborated. Could two of the three been dispatched to collect Penry's recently executed body, a mere three miles away, whilst the other stayed on watch?

SONNET 74

But be contented when that fell arrest
Without all bail shall carry me away;
My life hath in this line some interest,
Which for memorial still with thee shall stay.
When thou reviewest this, thou dost review
The very part was consecrate to thee.
The earth can have but earth, which is his due;
My spirit is thine, the better part of me.
So then thou hast but lost the dregs of life,
The prey of worms, my body being dead,
The coward conquest of a wretch's knife,
Too base of thee to be rememb'red.
The worth of that is that which it contains,
And that is this, and this with thee remains.

Sonnet 74, tells us three times, the poet is writing to the man responsible for faking his death.

1. *'Which for memorial still with thee shall stay…'*

2. *'The very part was consecrate to thee…'*

3. *'Too base of thee to be rememb'red.'*

In modern English:
1. 'Which you'll always have to remember me by.'
2. 'The precise part of me that was dedicated to you.'
3. 'Too worthless for you to remember.'

This sonnet sets out how the dramatist's death was faked and repeats sonnet 34's assertion that the dramatist was not the creator of his own death.

1. *But be contented when that fell arrest*

2. *Without all bail shall carry me away.*

Apparently, the poet's choice of 'Legal' rather than 'Religious' language, supports his authorship. He describes his death as a 'fell arrest' ('deadly arrest') because, it brought about his 'fictionalized death'.

Marlowe was arrested on May 20th and given bail to report daily to the Privy Council. On 30th he met his 'death'.

In line 'two' the scholars suggest that instead of bail the deadly arrest will carry him away. They say that this means 'into exile'.

The fact that the 'future tense - shall carry' is used instead of 'carried - in the past tense' is of considerable interest to some. It is believed that Marlowe intentionally used the future tense to escape identification. In other words if lines 1 & 2 were interpreted as follows:

But don't be upset when death arrives
To carry me off where no one can release me.

The poet is talking about a future occurrence otherwise he would have said:
And carried me off where no one could release me.

It is my intention now to deal with the rest of the sonnet giving an outline of what the scholars have had to say.

3. *My life hath in this line some interest*

4. *Which for memorial still with thee shall stay*

The Marlovian view is that the phrase 'in this line' is referring to the first full sentence of the sonnet and does not allude to the completed works of the poet.

It is argued he would have said 'these lines' if he meant that; both have the same amount of syllables.

The fourth line tells us it is being written to the man responsible for the poet's death. He (The poet) is confirming that the memory of the event will remain a secret between them. The use of the word 'still' suggests this sonnet was written sometime after Deptford and whilst in exile.

5. When thou reviewest this, thou dost review

6. *The very part was consecrate to thee,*

This is the second time the poet tells us the recipient is responsible for faking his death. We are about to learn the part played by this man in his 'death'. 'Consecrate's' meaning has been interpreted as 'to set apart as sacred' but the Marlovians believe it to be an echo of Sonnet 34's line 4: '*Hiding thy bravery in their rotten smoke*'. In other words, he gave of himself unreservedly and with devotion.

7. *The earth can have but earth, which is his due,*

8. *My spirit is thine, the better part of me.*

This tells us the poet is not buried in the grave. He is not quoting from 'The Common Book of Prayers' which mentions: 'earth to earth, ashes to ashes, dust to dust. He says: 'earth can have

BUT earth' meaning (possibly) it cannot have the body that came from earth.

This interpretation is supported by line 4 of Sonnet 112:

4. *So you are ore-greene my bad, my good allow*

My bad part is buried (ore-greene), my good part 'allowed' (alive) as is 'the better part' in line 8 above. This line 4 of sonnet 112 is also echoed in line 9 of the present sonnet (74) shown below.

9. *So then thou hast but lost the dregs of life,*

10. *The prey of worms, my body being dead,*

11. *The coward conquest of a wretches knife.*

12. *Too base of thee to be remembered.*

Again the interpretations flow and various meanings are attributed to single words or phrases. Nothing, it seems, is taken at face value by these scholars. For example a certain Duncan-Jones says that 'a wretches knife' is the abstract personification of Time's or Death's knife. I'm afraid I have no useful comment to make about that. The Marlovian version of lines 11 and 12 is:

The coward conquest of a wretches knife was too contemptible of you to be recalled.

There are some who argue the poet's life is too worthless to be remembered. The Marlovian view is it is not the poet's life, however, but the way in which Marlowe's death was staged, as stated in line 11, that was too base of the recipient to be remembered.

13. *The worth of that, is that which it contains,*

14. *And that is this, and this with thee remains.*

A general view is that the lines 13 and 14, above, mean: the worth of the dead body is the poetry it contained. (Note the past tense) The Marlovian's say 'The worth of that' refers to the fictional dead body mentioned above, for which the recipient was responsible. The only worth in faking his death is in what the fictional body contains. (Again note the present tense).This present tense tells us Marlowe is not really dead. What remains is Marlowe's literary compositions of which sonnets 34 and 74 are two examples.

Ed Note.

All the intelligent information above has been gleaned from:

The Christopher Marlowe library;

The Marlowe Society;

The Marlowe-Shakespeare connection;

Cynthia Morgan, concerning Marlowe's disgrace and Exile in the Shakespeare works;

The Shakespearean authorship Trust;

WGBH Educational Foundation (Much Ado about Something);

and Spark Notes LLC.

Apologies to Ms Duncan-Jones for missing the point.

Letter No. 14 - 18th April 2064

Dear Sir,

You will see from the date of this letter that the BIG day is rapidly approaching. As a matter of interest (to some), the 23rd of April was not only the date of WS's birth but also his death; but there were 52 years in between. So in five days' time, on the 23rd, we're celebrating his birth; 500 years ago.

Whilst I've been engaged researching the various theories and happenings, my team has been very active digging up the past. The Bard has been removed from his grave but nobody has been allowed to talk to him yet. The right side of his brain has been located and all the material gleaned, transferred into it. Although an Act of Congress would be required for me to reveal the actual method used, I am permitted to tell you that all the information was reduced to a micro dot and fired by the Neutron & Snapse Hypodermic Restorer, mentioned in Letter 7.

To the scientifically knowledgeable, I hasten to add that the hypodermic restorer and the 'micro dot' had to be quadruplicated to reach the four areas of the brain, selected in unison. We had to awaken and top-up the contents of WS's brain and accordingly the following sections were serviced: the AMYGDALA which stores emotional memory and fear conditioning, CEREBRAL CORTEX responsible for intelligence (short term memory not required so the PREFRONTAL CORTEX was not disturbed), HIPPOCAMPUS and BASAL GANGLIA were the final two sections implanted.

Before putting to use the vascular phase gun, the space satellite has to be in its correct co-ordinates. This will not happen until 0900 hours on the 23rd April. (I must try and find out WS's time of birth.) Everything else has been done: the grave digger sworn to secrecy and available to replant the Bard; the micro dot manufactured and implanted; the Ancient Hall of the Royal/Republican College of Surgeons booked and invitations, to nearly all English speaking countries World Wide, sent RSVP. (China the only country declining to attend on the grounds they have their own WS!)

I mentioned that the Micro Dot had already been implanted. What I didn't say, was it will take two days for all the information to be distributed and absorbed in the skull. We are not talking about any old-run of the mill micro dot; you know the one that a 1943, Second World War spy would attach to the back of a postage stamp! Paper/Silk or Pig Skin was not used in their manufacture. In this case tissue was extracted from WS's AMYGDALA and drenched with 'sound waves' carrying the information. The signs are good. No rejection of the implanted material has occurred. We are almost ready to go.

Before I question William Shakespeare I must prepare a lengthy plan of campaign. At this very moment in time his brain is being reminded/refreshed or surprised by the information fed into it. He has been given: a 'Time Line' of historical events leading up to his death; a list of 'Theories' relating to Marlowe's death; and arguments supporting 'Marlowe's Claim' to authorship of some or all WS's works.

All that is now required is to prepare for the interview with the knowledge that WS will only have, once the Vascular Filler phase gun has been fired, twenty minutes response time. But what a twenty minutes that will be. The world will be hanging on his every word. All electric traffic will stop. Communications will be turned to 'Extensive Brand' and the weather reports cancelled.

My next letter to you will contain the details of the interview to be held, culminating at 0900 hours on 25th April.
He will be told that if he figuratively nods his head a Static sound will imply an affirmative answer. Should he again THINK ONLY of shaking his head then two Static sounds will emanate.

(For example: Did you understand that? 'Static' = YES or 'Do you agree?' - 'Static - Static. = No.) This will give WS a clear 20 minutes to comment/answer or choke!

Drummond G Marvin

Letter No. 15 - 23rd April 2064

Dear Sir,

At last the dawn of the Big Day has arrived. My team and I are at present lodged in the Globe Theatre, on what used to be the river Thames' Embankment. I say used to be because the river has long since disappeared to accommodate heliports (all electric), rocket landing sites and other infrastructures. The Globe is in need of extensive restoration and it is hoped todays revelations will release the necessary funding.

Shakespeare has been re-housed in a lead-lined open coffin and is at present lying below the stage, directly underneath the trap door. He is due to rise at 0830 hours when the final proceedings will take place.

Hopefully the invited guests, seated in the comfort of the Great Circle and the representatives from television, radio and press taking up the standing room in the 'yard', will all have an experience of a life time.

'The outline of Marlowe's case', (see document 13) explains his followers' claim as to authorship; accordingly it has been implanted in WS's brain. He will be asked to comment, in support or otherwise, the various conspiracy theories revealed.

It is now 0830 hours and the coffin has slowly appeared from below. I had better explain, that to all intents and purposes, the incumbent is lifeless. There will be no activity to suggest otherwise, until 0900 hours when the satellite is in the correct co-ordinates; then WS's skull will appear to glow and humming noises will envelope the coffin. Questions and answers can then commence.

0845 has arrived and the 'Static Tester' is in place. The following test occurred:
Is your name William Shakespeare?
…Static…
We cannot print the 'Static – Static' reply as the question was too rude. Suffice to say the one Static affirmative confirmed the bones we were speaking to belonged to WS.

At 0850 after the applause has died down, I introduce myself to WS using a certain key on the console. I told him we were privileged to be at the 500 year anniversary of his birth. He has a once 'In a death-time' to put records straight. Did he write the Sonnets in their entirety? Does he agree that Sonnets 34 and 74 appear to support the Marlovian's contention that their candidate had his death faked for him to continue his literary career using 'Shakespeare' as a pen-name? Why did he not want publication of the Sonnets?

It is now 0859 and when I say 'over to you Will' you have twenty minutes to give us your carefully considered reply.

The whole of the Anglo/American world is waiting with bated breath to hang on your every word.

WHAT HAVE YOU GOT TO SAY ABOUT ALL THE CONSPIRACY THEORIES AND ALLEGATIONS MPLANTED IN YOUR CONSCIOUSNESS?

What do you make of it all?

Over to you, Will.

Shakespeare's Reply

"BOLLOCKS!"

…Static…Static…Static…

FIN

Ed. Note

Old and Middle English refer to 'Bollocks' as: 'Beallucas' or 'Ballokes'.

Either way, Shakespeare now can be said to have known 66,535 words!

Acknowledgement

I would like to thank my wife, Betty, for her loyal support during the writing of my book.

Other Works from the Author

An enthusiastic member of **Writers Ink** - a writers group which meets monthly in Playa Flamenca, Costa Blanca, Spain, Drummond has contributed to their anthologies:

Talk of the Towns
Food Glorious Food
Precinct Murder
Des Res
Of Course I Believe in Father Christmas

Drummond has also compiled and published a Criminal Law Training Manual for Police Forces in the Caribbean.

A Request from Drummond G Marvin

My Dear Friends,

I sincerely hope you have enjoyed my book.
If so, would you spare a few minutes to write a short review?
I am sure you know how much it means to an author to receive favourable reviews, and I thank you for your support.

Drummond G Marvin

Printed in Dunstable, United Kingdom